D0179099

First published in paperback in Great Britain by HarperCollins Children's Books in 2010
This edition published in 2014

1 3 5 7 9 10 8 6 4 2

iSBN: 978-0-00-812629-2

HarperCollins Children's Books is a division of HarperCollins Publishers Ltd.

Text and illustrations copyright © Sebastien Braun 2010, 2014

Visit our website at: www.harpercollins.co.uk

Printed and bound in italy

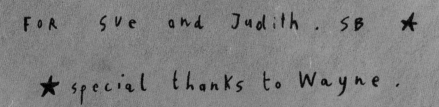

FOR Sue and Judith. SB ★

★ special thanks to Wayne.

Toot and Pop!

by Sebastien Braun

HarperCollins *Children's Books*

Toot!

Toot!

Toot!

This is Toot. Hello, Toot!
He is a very strong little tugboat.

Every day Toot works in the harbour,
pulling all the big, heavy loads.

"Heave-ho!"

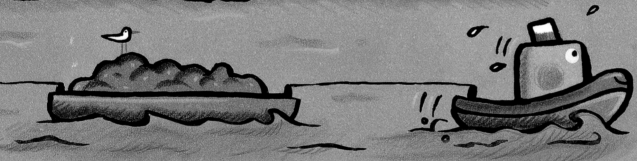

One day, a brand new boat was going
to be launched at the harbour.

Toot couldn't wait to see it. He rushed off to the dock...

and what a boat it was!

Huge waves swirled behind him, rocking and knocking all the boats into one another. "Watch out!" screamed Lenny the lighthouse. But it was too late...

Pop went straight into the sea wall and came to a stop. His engine was broken.

The harbour master
came rushing out.
"Silly Pop!" he said.
"Look what you've done."

"He wouldn't wait
for Toot," said Lenny.

"Well, now you'll just have
to let Toot take you back to
the dock to be mended," the
harbour master told Pop crossly.

No sooner had he spoken,
than Toot came rushing
to the rescue.

Soon Pop was settled in the dock, ready to be fixed.
"I'm sorry, Toot," he said. "I should have let you do your job.
Please will you help me when I'm back in the water?"

"Of course I will," said Toot kindly...

"That's what friends are for!"

Toot sailed happily back
across the harbour.
"Well done, Toot!" said Lenny.

Toot

Toot

Toot

"It's all in a day's work," said Toot.